Feather

by Cao Wenxuan

Illustrated by Roger Mello

Translated from the Chinese
by Chloe Garcia Roberts

*elsewhere
editions*

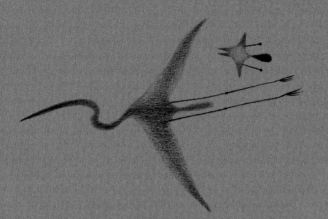

One day a great wind blew through Beijing. As I was walking into the gale I suddenly noticed a single white feather on the ground go fluttering and floating up into the sky. The higher it flew the farther it went. The feather was riding the wind with grace and ease yet at the same time precariously and helplessly. At that moment a strange thought occurred to me: *Where did this tiny feather come from? Where did it want to go? Could this feather be searching for its source?*

I believe a good picture book comes very close to philosophy. In the story, Feather flies up into the sky and begins relentlessly pondering the question: *Exactly what kind of bird do I come from?* With each type of bird she comes in contact with (Kingfisher, Cuckoo, Heron, Peacock, etc.), Feather asks the same question over and over again: *Am I yours?* The character choices and the circular repetitive structure are both designed for children. However underlying this simple story of Feather pondering her questions are actually the core questions of human thought: Where do I come from? Where do I want to go? Who do I belong to? In fact, Feather's journey of riding the wind, her journey of questioning, is really the human journey of searching for a sense of belonging .

Cao Wenxuan

"*É um pássaro no céu, é um pássaro no chão*. (A bird in the sky, a bird on the ground)," sings Brazilian maestro Tom Jobim. There are feathers that protect, feathers designed to fly, feathers that warm the bodies of busy birds with tenderness. There are feathers through which not even the smallest drop of water can trespass. Don't mistake one feather for another, for no two are the same. When Leonardo da Vinci was a baby, he felt the feathers of a hawk brushing his mouth, and this dreamlike vision made his imagination soar. When my friends Mingzhou Zhang and Ahmad Redza showed me *Feather* written by Cao Wenxuan, I realized that I was meant to illustrate the philosophy in between his words. So I fell in love with Wenxuan's story. A bird from China, a bird from Brazil. In a dream, Tom Jobim said to me: don't forget to draw a spoonbill. In the Egyptian Book of the Dead, personality is measured by comparing the weight of one's heart to the weight of a feather. For it must be as strong as it is light. Just like a great poem, just like a great story.

Roger Mello

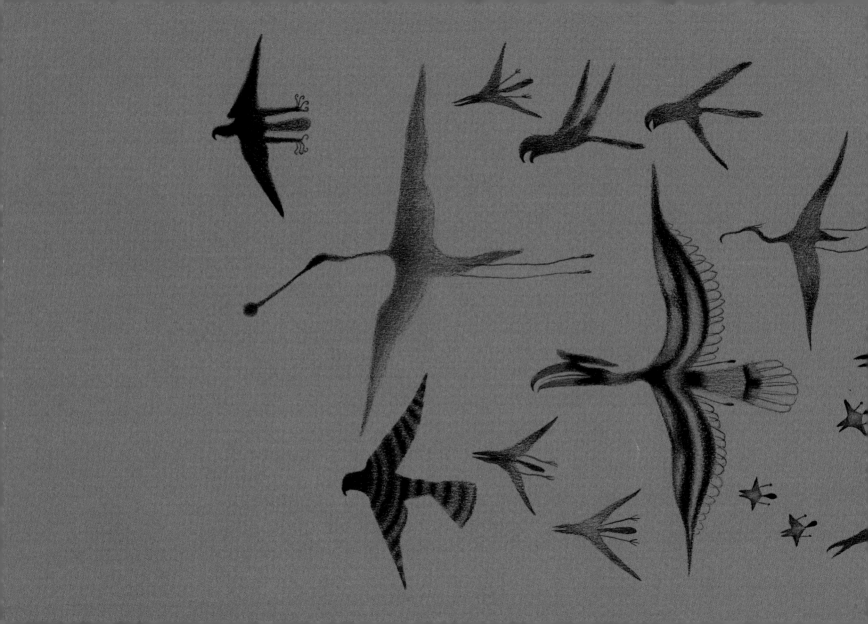

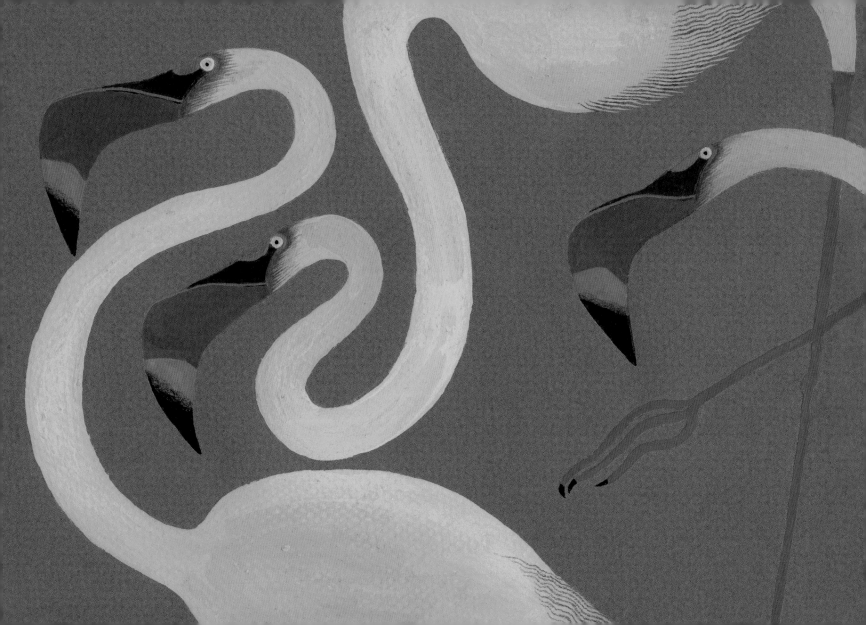

A single feather was blown a little while this way by the wind and a little while that way by the wind.

And when there was no wind, which sometimes happened for days at a time, she would wait in a tuft of wild grass or a pile of fallen leaves, all alone.

One day, a little boy and a little girl walked by Feather. They picked her up and passed her back and forth looking at her.

When they threw her back to the ground and started to walk away, Feather heard the little girl ask the little boy, "What kind of bird is that feather from?"

Yes, what kind of bird do I belong to? thought Feather. And from that moment on, she began to ask herself that question all the time.

A strong burst of wind came along and blew Feather up into the sky.

The feeling of fluttering high in the air was delightful.

If I belonged to a bird, I could fly even higher! she thought.

How she longed for the sky! How she longed to soar!

Feather drifted down onto a tree by the waterside.

A kingfisher was perched there on a branch, head tilted, silently watching the water's surface.

Feather shyly asked the kingfisher, "Am I yours?"

The kingfisher did not respond to her and suddenly plunged into the water. After a moment, it flew back up with a small silvery fish still wriggling in its mouth.

The kingfisher flew to the tree branch again, and again tilting its head, sat silently watching the water's surface.

Feather asked the kingfisher over and over, "Am I yours?"

But the kingfisher was so focused on catching fish it completely ignored her.

Feather waited silently.

At long last, when the kingfisher was no longer busy, it turned its head, took a long look at Feather and said, "You are not mine."

A strong burst of wind came along and blew Feather up into the sky.

A cuckoo flew by alongside her.

"Am I yours?" Feather inquired.

The cuckoo was so focused on calling out *cuckoo, cuckoo* to people that it didn't pay any attention to Feather.

The wind kept blowing and Feather kept floating in the sky.

When the cuckoo came flying back around, Feather once again inquired, "Am I yours?"

The cuckoo turned its head, took a long look, and said, "Not mine! Not mine!"

Feather drifted down by the side of a pond.

In the shallow water was a heron looking for food.

Feather asked the heron, "Am I yours?"

The heron, focused on continuing its search, paid no attention to her.

After a little while, the heron walked back over.

Feather once again inquired, "Am I yours?"
The heron took a long look at Feather and replied, "You aren't mine."

A strong burst of wind came and once again blew Feather up into the sky.

A flock of wild geese flew by.

Feather asked the leader of the flock, "Am I yours?" but the goose was so focused on guiding the others onward it didn't answer Feather.

As the flock flew by they created a strong gust of air and Feather was swept along, tumbling and rolling, but she still didn't stop asking, "Am I yours? Am I yours?"

The wild goose flying at the very end of the flock responded, "Little one, you are not one of our wild goose feathers."

"I knew it." Feather said quietly. And by the time she could float steadily in the air again, the ranks of wild geese were already long gone.

Feather drifted down into a wide grassy meadow.

A blue peacock was just then spreading open its tail.

Several people gathered to watch—it was truly beautiful!

After a while, the peacock folded up its multicolor show and the people scattered.

Feather asked the peacock, "Am I yours?"

The peacock took a long look at Feather and said, "You are really very impertinent asking me 'Am I yours?' Perhaps you haven't looked carefully enough, my feathers are without a doubt the most beautiful in the world!"

Feather, hidden in a tuft of grass, didn't make a sound.

Later Feather asked a magpie,
"Am I yours?"

She asked a swan, "Am I yours?"

She asked a mallard, "Am I yours?"

She asked a lyrebird and a lark,
"Am I yours?"

The answer was always the same,
"You are not."

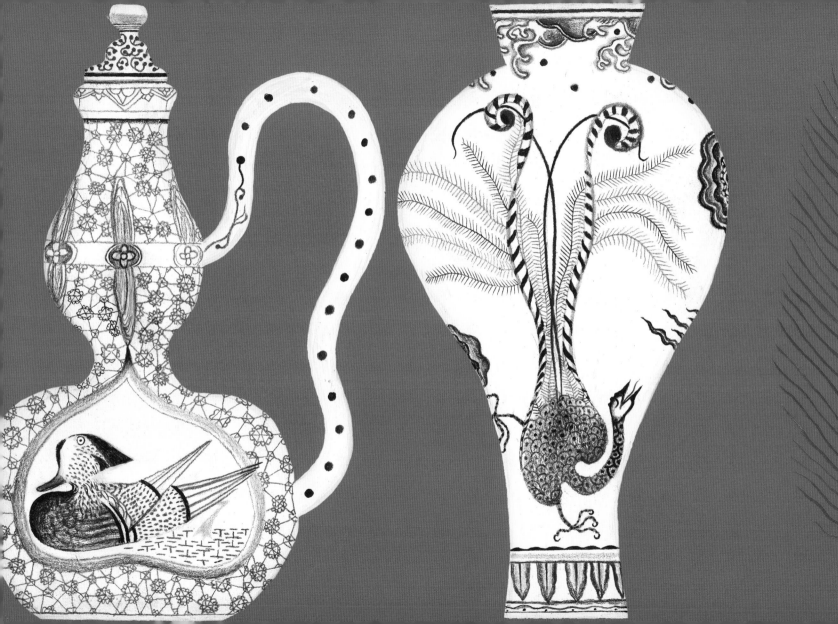

One day Feather came upon a kind-hearted skylark.

The skylark said to her, "Little one, even though you don't belong to me I will still grant your wish and take you flying way up into the sky because I am without a doubt the highest-flying bird in the world!"

Holding Feather in its beak, the skylark flew vigorously upwards through the endless sea of clouds and carried her to the highest spot in the sky.

The skylark released Feather and the two of them floated together in the air.

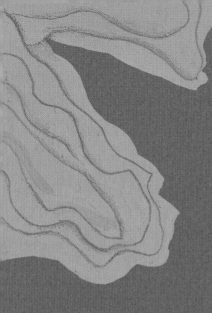

Feather drifted down on top of a mountain peak.

On the cliff, a fierce hawk sat perched.

Feather didn't have any reason to think she might belong to this hawk. She thought for a moment and then, unsure if it was because of her excitement or the gentle wind flowing by, she approached, trembling.

"Am I yours?" Feather asked in a small voice.

"What?" asked the hawk and tilted its head a little.

"Am I yours?" Feather asked again in her loudest voice.

The hawk didn't answer Feather. It crouched down and slowly unfolded its gigantic wings. A skylark came flying towards them.

Feather said to the hawk, "I know that skylark…"

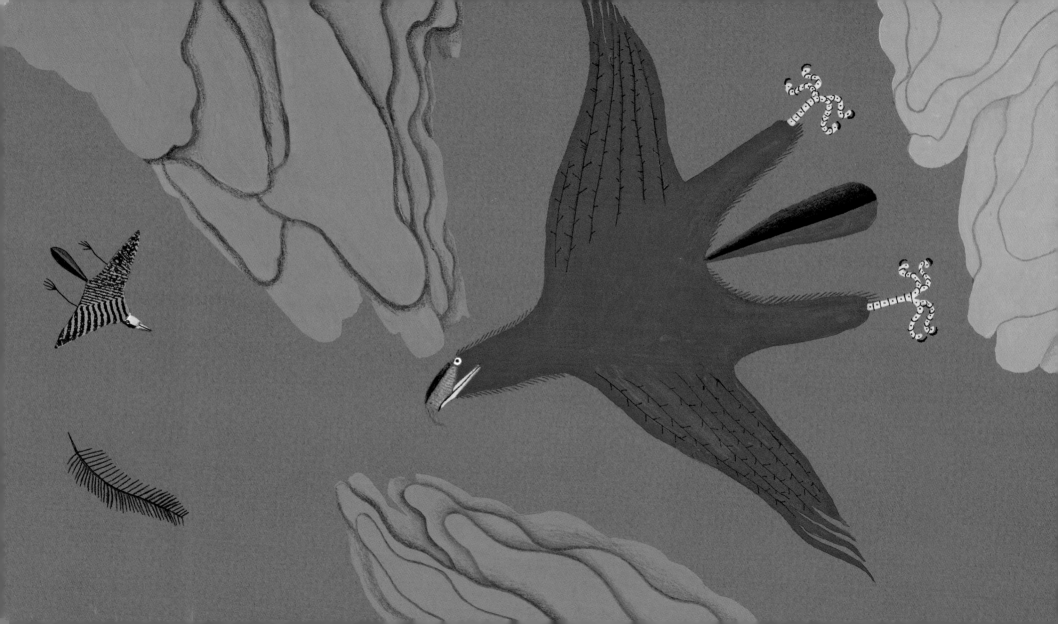

She hadn't even finished speaking when she saw the hawk fly off the cliff with a whoosh and shoot like a black arrow towards the skylark.

Feather heard the sound of a scream in the air and saw a drop of bright red blood like a glittering bead drip down from the sky.

Oh wind! Come quickly! Come quickly and blow me away! Feather said, silently in her heart because she was unable to make a sound.

The wind came and Feather flew upwards, spinning above the gorge. Then she floated down toward the fields at the foot of the mountain.

From out of the sky a rain began to fall. The raindrops slid off Feather like tears.

As long as I live, Feather thought, *I never want to see that hawk again!*

Feather drifted down into a field.

She lay in a tuft of grass, thinking nothing. She lay like that for several days.

Then one day in the brilliant sunshine, a mother hen came along with her flock of little chicks, foraging. The whole family was happy, joyful, and carefree.

Feather thought, *Ah! To walk upon the earth instead of flying up in the sky can also be wonderful!*

She very much wanted to ask the mother hen, Am I yours? But she had no courage left.

Then under the warm sun the mother hen slowly unfolded her wings, and…
Oh! It looks like she is missing a single feather!

Cao Wenxuan is one of China's most prolific and popular authors, publishing over 100 works, including novels, short stories, essays, and picture books. He is a professor of literature at Peking University as well as the Vice-President of the Beijing Writer's Association. Cao has received the Hans Christian Andersen Award, the Chinese National Book Award, and the Golden Butterfly Award of the Tehran International Film Festival.

Roger Mello has illustrated over 100 titles – 22 of which he also wrote. Mello has won numerous awards for writing and illustrating, including three of IBBY's Luis Jardim Awards, the Best Children's Book International Award, and the Hans Christian Andersen Award. He is the author and illustrator of *You Can't Be Too Careful!*, translated by Daniel Hahn.

Chloe Garcia Roberts is the translator of Li Shangyin's *Derangements of My Contemporaries: Miscellaneous Notes*, which was awarded a PEN / Heim Translation Fund Grant, and the author of a book of poetry, *The Reveal*. She lives in Boston and is the managing editor for the *Harvard Review*.

Text Copyright © Cao Wenxuan

Illustration Copyright © Roger Mello

First published in China by China Children's Press and Publication Group

All Rights Reserved

羽毛

文字版权©曹文轩

图画版权©罗杰·米罗

由中国少年儿童新闻出版总社在中国首次出版

所有权利保留

English language translation © Chloe Garcia Roberts, 2017

First Elsewhere Editions Printing, 2017

Library of Congress Cataloging-in-Publication Data Available Upon Request

Elsewhere Editions 232 3rd Street #A111 Brooklyn, NY 11215 www.elsewhereeditions.org

Distributed by Penguin Random House

www.penguinrandomhouse.com

This publication was made possible with support from Lannan Foundation, the New York State Council on the Arts, a state agency, the National Endowment for the Arts, Amazon Literary Partnership, and the New York City Department of Cultural Affairs.

ART WORKS. · National Endowment for the Arts · NYCULTURE · NEW YORK STATE OF OPPORTUNITY | Council on the Arts · amazon literary partnership

PRINTED IN CHINA